KATHERINE H. BROWN

White Chocolate, Weapons, & A Walk Down the Aisle

Ooey Gooey Bakery Mystery Book 5

First published by Katherine Brown Books 2021

This novel is entirely a work of fiction. The names, characters and incidents portrayed in it are the work of the author's imagination. Any resemblance to actual persons, living or dead, events or localities is entirely coincidental.

First edition

ISBN: 978-1-7337258-9-7

This book was professionally typeset on Reedsy.
Find out more at reedsy.com

Contents

1

Chapter 1

"Landon proposed. Again."

"What?" I screeched, dropping the bowl of nuts-about-chocolate cookie dough I held. It bounced and spun across the counter like a top before Victoria stopped it.

Sam blushed but nodded, her sleek ponytail bouncing and showing off her newest highlights, rose gold. It was the tamest color her hair had been in years. She held out her hand and a large diamond winked up at me, almost as bright as her smile.

Victoria and BeeBee squealed and clapped.

Gladys only smirked. "It's about dang time he quit lollygagging around."

"Let me see the ring, let me see!" Victoria grasped Sam's hand and whipped out her phone. "I have got to send Millie a picture of this. Do you mind?"

"Send away."

Landon and Sam had been dating for months. Technically, he'd asked him to marry her already but they had put it off in favor of dating longer.

I figured that Landon had been waiting to have a decent home ready before getting married because anyone could see they were head over heels for each other from the start. They worked together to renovate an old beach house that he'd bought and had only recently finished it.

I looked around the kitchen of the Ooey Gooey Goodness Bakery, our usual hangout even when the baking was finished. The whole crew was here, everyone but Millie who had moved away to pursue an art degree. Victoria and BeeBee gushed about how romantic the proposal must have been and you could tell they were already daydreaming about their own prince charming coming one day.

"Congratulations!! Does that mean you are finally setting a wedding date this time?" I asked my best friend.

Biting her bottom lip first, Sam said, "That's the thing. We actually plan to have it at Landon's house, or technically the beach in front of what will be our house, in two weeks."

"Two weeks?" Gladys and I shouted together.

Sam nodded. "We don't want to wait until the busy holiday season. And besides, we aren't inviting a ton of people." With a shrug, she smiled. "It'll be fine."

"Fine?" I snapped, waving my arms around. "What do you mean fine? This is your wedding; it should be better than fine!" I couldn't believe it. This was literally the last thing I expected. I mean, come on. Sam and a scaled-down, intimate wedding? Sam of the designer clothes, Southern-bred sophistication, and high-heels?

"Piper, I promise. This is exactly what I want," she assured me with a hand on my shoulder. "The five-star destination wedding would have been my mother's idea. Besides, what better destination than the beach that has captured all of our best memories and the home that will be storing our future ones?"

She had a point.

Not sure that I really wanted to know the answer to my next question, I had to ask. I lowered my voice. "Are your parents invited?"

"No." Her mouth tightened and her eyes grew sad. It was one of the only signs of how upset she still was with them. Sam and her mother had always been on rocky terms. Deidra Lowe cared only for power and appearances and was disappointed when the children she groomed to further her own aspirations decided to live their own lives instead. That wasn't the worst though. The straw that broke the camel's back came when secrets about her past revealed the depth of lows that Deidra would go to for money and maintaining her image. Sam and her parents hadn't spoken since that disastrous night when a half-brother Sam and Griff didn't know about showed up and tried to kill Deidra for breaking his father's heart years ago.

Gladys pulled me out of my reverie when she threw her hands up across the room and grumbled. "Two weeks, you say? How do you expect me to put together a decent bachelorette party in two weeks? Who do you think I am, Houdini?" With more mumbles and shakes of her head, she collected her purse and headed out the back door without so much as a see you later.

I locked the door back behind her and laughed. "Oh boy."

Sam grinned. "Well, that could get interesting."

"Let's get down to business," I straightened at the counter, pulling a notebook and pen from my apron pocket. I rarely went anywhere without my notebook. "There's only one thing I really need to know. Wedding cake?" She'd asked for red velvet before, but a girl has a right to change her mind; I might as well double check.

The next hour we spent discussing cake flavors, desserts, and the number of guests all while we baked cookies, brownies, and a few truffles for today's menu in the bakery café.

I also rang up Flo next door who readily agreed to provide a bouquet and a few smaller flower arrangements for the seating area on the beach. "They'll be my gift," she insisted.

With food and flowers accounted for, we only needed to think about the reception decorations.

"Please, can we do them?" BeeBee begged.

Victoria nodded. "It's the least we can do. I mean, I know we will help with some of the desserts but really, since you're doing the cake, Piper, we will have more free time than you."

"That's great for me girls," Sam agreed. "I'll get you a key to the house closer to the wedding so you can come and go as you need to set up everything."

"Should I call Gladys and see what she's plotting?" I wondered.

Sam waved a hand. "No. Let's let her make it a surprise. You know how she enjoys surprises."

"Oh, does she! But will we enjoy the surprise as much as she does? It could be way out of hand." I had to point out.

"I'm sure it will be fine," Sam insisted.

Famous last words, I thought to myself.

2

Chapter 2

ONE WEEK LATER

"Do you hear that, Piper?"

I cocked my head. Sure enough, I heard the noise that had caught Sam's attention. "Who in the world would be banging on the café door at this time of morning?"

"Whoever it is, they must be desperate for a fix," she joked.

My best friend Sam and I owned and operated the Ooey Gooey Goodness Bakery. If someone outside needed a muffin at four in the morning, she was right. They must be desperate.

"I'll check it out." I wiped stray trails of honey onto a kitchen towel.

The towel lost the battle with my now thoroughly sticky hands as the banging grew more insistent.

Before I could cross the kitchen, a new sound rang out. Three ominous pops made me jump. I looked at Sam, catching her wide-eyed glance. We bolted through the swinging door and into the café at the front of the bakery. It only occurred to me as I unlocked the front door that the knocking had stopped.

"Maybe we shouldn't open it," Sam whispered.

"Probably not."

"But you aren't going to stop…."

I hesitated. Everything was now quiet. I drew in a calming breath. "Nope." I eased the door open, silently cursing the tinkling noise the bell above made. Nobody stood on the other side and I sighed in relief.

Sam leaned over my shoulder. "Well?"

Turning back inside, I shrugged. "Nobody there."

From somewhere in the dark, a faint moan belied my words. My stomach clenched. It sounded like something or someone was in pain. Steeling myself, I opened the door wider and stepped out. Sam stayed right on my heels. Her heels, tall spikes that had no place in a bakery but somehow worked for Sam, clicked along the sidewalk, were the only noise as we searched for the source of the moan.

Midway between the bakery and Flo's Flowers, I saw a dark shape lying next to the tall trash can in the middle of the sidewalk. "Sam, over here."

Huddled together, we crept slowly forward. Another moan sounded, followed by a sputtering cough. Sam switched on the flashlight app of her phone and for a moment I really wished she hadn't. A man in a gray leather coat clutched his chest, his fingers doing little to stop the flow of dark red liquid.

"Call 911!" I yelled at Sam. Ripping my apron over my head, I wadded it into a ball and pushed it tightly against where the most blood seemed to be coming from. If television were at all accurate, I didn't think it would do much good. The man's breathing was raspy, shallow; blood trickled from his nose and mouth.

"Package," he spoke with effort, nearly giving me a heart attack.

I leaned closer. "What?"

"Package." Cough. "Package for Gladys." With a small shudder, his hand fell limp and his breathing ceased.

"The ambulance is on the way."

Sam's voice sounded far away. It barely registered that she was talking to me until her heels made their way into my peripheral vision.

"Piper? Did you hear me?" She repeated herself. "The ambulance is coming."

I shook my head. "I don't think it matters."

"What?"

I stood slowly. "He's dead. At least, I think he's dead." My head felt like it was spinning. "Am I supposed to check for a pulse or something?" A cacophony of noise sounded. Saved by the sirens. In less than a minute, paramedics were rushing over. Sam gently helped me up and we moved out of the way.

3

Chapter 3

When the officer began to ask the same questions over again, I couldn't take it anymore. My hands were cold, so cold they were starting to go numb. My head hurt. And my thoughts were flying every which way since the dead man had seemed to be talking about my friend Gladys during his last moments on Earth.

"Miss Rivers," the voice said again.

I looked up at the officer. Officer Jack, according to his name tag, frowned at me but I didn't really care. "I don't know anything else and I'm freezing. If you think of new questions later, feel free to come find me in the bakery." I pointed over my shoulder. "I'll be here all day."

I vaguely heard Sam apologizing to the officer, then the tell-tell click of heels that meant she was right behind me.

I held the door open for Sam, then twisted the lock behind us.

"I'll get the cookies," she said simply.

Cookies may not fix everything but our motto was that they went a long way toward making it better.

Not trusting myself to speak, I pulled out a chair at one of the small round café tables and sat down. Not even the lively and artistically depicted scene of dancing desserts that decorated the tabletop could cheer me.

Sam returned bearing not only a plate of cookies, but two glasses of tea as well.

"Chocolate chunk and hazelnut for you, mocha peppermint chip for me."

"Peppermint doesn't belong in chocolate."

Sam laughed. "Yes, you've been telling me that for years." Sobering, she peered closer at me. "Are you okay?"

I whooshed out a breath. "That man. He said something when he died."

"Really? I didn't hear you say anything about that to the police. Should I go get Officer Jack?"

I shook my head. Biting into a cookie, I drew strength from the deep chocolate flavor. I've always thought that chocolate might be my actual blood type. "No. I didn't tell him and I don't think I want to. At least, not yet."

Sam frowned. "I don't understand."

"That's the problem; neither do I. The man said *package for Gladys* right before he died." It was bad enough I had to witness a person slip from this life right in front of my eyes. But for it to be someone gunned down violently in the street? And for that same person to bring up another of my best friends? What did it mean? How could he know Gladys? I gave my head a shake. There were just too many questions.

"Gladys?" Sam's eyes widened. "Are you sure?"

"Yeah, that's what he said."

Noises from the kitchen made me look up.

Sam stood. "It must be BeeBee or Victoria. What should we tell them?"

"The minimum for now. How about we see if they can handle the baking while we make a fast trip out to see Gladys?"

The girls were more than happy to take care of things, and lucky for everyone Eva was in town visiting her sister so BeeBee and Victoria had extra hands this morning.

Only fifteen minutes later, we stood on the doorstep of Gladys's bright yellow bungalow.

I knocked.

"What in the world are you two doing standing on the steps like strangers?" Gladys said as she pulled open the door. "You should know by now you're both family, and family can come on in."

We followed Gladys into the living room. Muting the TV, she offered us a drink. "Can I get you some tea? Or cider?"

"Cider sounds delicious," Sam licked her lips.

"Thanksgiving and Christmas are still a bit far out for cider for me. Tea sounds wonderful though, extra ice."

"Back in a jiff," she said.

I settled onto the couch next to Sam, debating how exactly to ask Gladys about the man who spoke of a package for her. Especially since I hadn't seen any package anywhere near him.

"So, what brings you two here and away from the bakery?" Gladys asked right away.

So much for gathering my thoughts.

"Well, the thing is, I wondered if you were expecting any packages lately?"

Gladys leaned back in her recliner and considered. "Maybe two or three. Why?" The she slapped her knee. "I bet y'all are trying to figure out what we're doing for the bachelorette party this weekend. Is that it? Nope, not telling, no way."

Sam shook her head. "Actually, that's not it at all."

"The thing is," I started slowly, "a man outside the bakery this morning said something strange about a package for you."

"Strange how?"

"Well, strange because it was the last thing he said before he died."

"Died?" Gladys yelped.

"Mm-hmm," Sam nodded. "Right there on the sidewalk, practically in Piper's arms."

Gladys harumphed. "Somebody better start at the beginning of this story."

Just as I was wrapping up the telling of our horrifying morning, Sam lurched to the TV remote and turned up the volume. "Oh my gosh! Piper, Gladys, look! It's on TV. The murder by the bakery is on the news." We all stopped to listen.

'In the wee hours of the morning, J.D. Sweets was found shot to death on Main Street. Sweets, a small-time go-between for the larger criminal minds stretching across three counties. was known by his nickname Sweets Deals to local law enforcement; his rap sheet had him pegged as a broker for deals, mover of money, and running pick-up and delivery services for illegal goods when parties did not want to meet. In a stunning revelation from an inside source working the case, Sweets is suspected to have been working for arms dealers when he met his end today. Our source is telling us that a large duffle bag of weapons was found tossed in the garbage can adjacent to Sweets' body.

The news broke for a commercial. For a few moments, we all stared at the screen and then each other. I had no idea what to think. *Arms dealers? Criminal organizations? Here? In Seashell Bay?* There had to be a mistake. That was all my fuzzy brain kept telling me. Some bizarre mistake that weapons, a dead body, and a supposed package for Gladys were appearing in our typically quiet little beach town.

Okay, granted. There had been that one kidnapping mishap. And maybe a small leg of human traffickers tried to make their way into the surrounding areas. The attempted murder of Deidra didn't even count; I mean, tons of people wished her dead.

Gladys spoke, interrupting my turbulent thoughts.

"I think we may have a problem. Two problems, actually."

"What?" I asked despite the feeling that I really wouldn't like the answer.

"First, I know him. Sort of. Second, I bet the smoke bombs I ordered for the bachelorette party aren't coming now."

4

Chapter 4

"Know him how?"

"Smoke bombs?"

"Start talking," I put my glass of tea down. With Gladys, God bless her, having nothing that you could drop or break in shock was always the safer plan.

"Alright, alright. It's going to spoil the surprise though."

I frowned, numbering things on my fingers. "Dead man. Weapons. Smoke bombs. This is one surprise I'd rather have all the details on up front."

"Agreed," Sam nodded.

"Party poopers." She held up her hands to stifle any further complaints.

"Well, I knew you two weren't going to want to go out to a bar or a club and some people who remain nameless but are sitting in this room seem to think I'm a little past the age for those types of shenanigans, so, I decided to buy some black lights, and smoke machines, and balloons, and hire a funky musician from somewhere and just have our own little party with all of the best party elements but none of the drinking or bad decisions."

"What happened?" I ignored a series of text message noises coming from my phone.

"And how did this Sweets character play into it?" Sam prodded.

"I'm getting to that," Gladys assured us. Downing another swallow of tea, she continued. "None of the smoke machines that I found online said they would deliver in time for the party. I thought maybe there was a smaller option so I just kept typing in things to that Google search bar. I was clicking and clicking all around but nothing sounded right; there were smoker grills and smoke tubes for food, all kinds of things. I figured I'd try one or two more links before calling it quits but the next thing that I clicked put me on a page showing that I had added a hand-sized smoke grenade to my cart." She shrugged. "That sounded pretty small so I added four more. A little bit later I received an email saying cash would be due when the order was delivered."

Is it possible for your eyes to pop out of your head? I've read about it, but is it a thing? Because I'm pretty sure mine were on the verge if so.

"Smoke grenades? Gladys, smoke grenades are not the same things as smoke bombs."

"Well, it looks like now we know how a weapons dealer got involved."

I shook my head. "I still don't understand how that translates to a guy showing up to the bakery with a bag of guns."

"I can't rightly say about the guns, but I did use the bakery address for delivery. They said no post office boxes."

I gaped.

Sam burst into laughter.

"We are going to need a list of everything you ordered for the party," I told Gladys.

"Are you sure? I mean, something has to be a surprise."

Loud banging sounded at the front door.

Gladys excused herself to answer it. I took the chance to read my missed messages.

"Uh-oh," I groaned.

"What?" Sam asked. "What now?"

"Hey, Gladys," I called. "I don't think you should open that door."

Too late.

5

Chapter 5

"Gladys Hill?" A uniformed officer with his hand on his holstered weapon asked the moment she opened the door.

"Yes?" After her disastrous and short marriage to Frederic, Gladys changed her name back to her first married name.

"I need you to come with me to answer some questions in an investigation concerning illegal weapons dealing."

"You knew the police were coming?" Sam whispered, slapping me on the shoulder.

"Victoria texted. They've been to the bakery already."

She smacked me on the shoulder. "That warrants more than 'uh-oh', don't you think?"

I stuck my tongue out at her.

The officer cleared his throat and Gladys took that as her opportunity to speak.

"I have a big pitcher of tea made and would be happy to answer all of your questions here." She smiled sweeter than the tea itself but no dice.

"Ma'am, I'm afraid I need you to come with me. Now." He glanced to Sam and me again. "Who are you two?"

"Friends of Gladys," Sam stood. "Does she need a lawyer?"

"Can we come with her?" I added.

The officer declined us both with a single head shake. "Just standard procedure. No charges are being pressed at this. You can follow and wait to pick her up if you like but Gladys will be questioned alone."

"What a mess," I remarked as Sam and I parked in the visitor's lot at the police department twenty minutes later.

"No kidding." Sam chewed on her lip. "What I don't understand is how they hit on Gladys as a person of interest so quickly. You didn't tell them about her name being mentioned."

"Don't know. We'll have to ask her when she's released."

"If she's released," Sam corrects.

The silence stretched. "Admit it. I was right."

Sam raised her brows. "Right about what?"

"About Gladys and the bachelorette party being a risky idea."

She sighed. "You were right. But even you couldn't have predicted potential weapons charges."

"Nope."

"Do we tell Victoria and BeeBee?"

"Might as well. We may need them to cover more shifts at the bakery depending on how things go. I'll text them."

Sam nodded. "Okay. What about the guys? Do we tell them?"

My mind raced at the thought. *They would lock us all up until the wedding. Maybe longer.* "No way," I said.

She laughed. "Come on, Piper. We have to."

"Grr." I growled in her direction. "Then why did you make not telling them an option?"

"To see your face when you thought about it."

This time, I slugged her in the arm.

Half an hour later, Sam pointed to the front of the building. "Look, there's Gladys now."

"No handcuffs. That's a good sign."

Gladys climbed into the back seat. "I'm starving. Let's go to the bakery."

I can't even judge her. My stomach is growling and that sounds like a fantastic plan. Besides, Victoria and BeeBee are probably dying to hear all of the details, too. "Sounds good but then we have some more talking to do."

"I know, I know." Gladys shuffled her purse around in her lap. "Back in my day, there wasn't this much fuss over trying to plan a simple party."

Simple. Ha. Gladys kept us on our toes but her genuine care for people and zest for life made every agonizing second of craziness worth it. I looked at Sam's small smile and knew she was thinking the same thing.

6

Chapter 6

My alarm clock beeped. A highly annoying beep. I'd have to think about changing the sound.

Usually, I'm up before my alarm but I hadn't been able to fall asleep last night. The afternoon before had passed in a blur. Over slices of pie, Gladys had filled us all in on how her questioning session had gone. The police obtained the bakery address and her name from a scrap of paper the deceased man had in his pockets. From there, the girls had quickly given the officers Gladys's home address and tried to text and give us a heads up.

I stretched and groaned. I still had a lingering headache from thinking about all of it last night. Oh well. Time to get to work.

At the Ooey Gooey Goodness Bakery, I found more than our normal crew waiting for me. "Eva! What a surprise!" I hugged BeeBee's younger sister with genuine pleasure. It was so wonderful to see them reunited after finding out what a horrific childhood the girls had suffered.

"When I got the wedding invitation, I decided to surprise everyone and come a few days early. I thought maybe you could all use some extra hands.

"You bet we could."

Sam's head bobbed up and down. "You bet. We never turn down help."

"Especially now that we have a new mystery to solve." Gladys grinned ear to ear.

"NO." I waved my arms in a big X motion. "No, we are not solving a murder. Not again. And especially not on the week of Sam's wedding."

"Of course not, silly."

I eyed Gladys. She never gives up easily. "Then what mystery could we possibly have to solve?"

"The location of my smoke bombs and how to get my name cleared off the police radar."

Sam stepped in this time, arms crossed and eyes blazing. "Smoke grenades. You ordered military grade smoke grenades and I'm pretty sure we told you that those are a no-go for this party or any other."

It wasn't often that Sam put that high-heeled foot of hers down, but when she did, she was a force.

"Exactly why we should find them."

"Wait. What?" I swear, Gladys sometimes made about as much sense as a swimsuit in a snowstorm.

"So that nobody else gets their hands on them. I'd feel just terrible to hear of some bank robbery or convenience store stick-up involving smoke grenades and knowing it was my fault they were just rattling around town somewhere." Gladys sat down in a chair and covered her heart with a trembling hand.

My eyes narrowed. "Have you been taking acting classes at the senior's theater program?"

She clapped her hands. "Oh, you can tell! So, I'm really getting good at conveying that genuine emotion like they talk about then?"

Victoria coughed into her apron to cover a laugh.

From her wide-eyed stare and the steel grip she had on BeeBee's arm, it looked like Eva didn't know what to think. I'd forgotten that she probably didn't know about all the arms dealing, illegal weapon buying, dead guys, and Gladys being in the middle of it to boot.

"Girls, why don't y'all go open up the café a few minutes early. I think we can handle the last of the baking." I smiled extra-wide at Eva, probably looking less reassuring than I hoped.

Once they were all out of earshot, I tried reasoning again with Gladys. "I don't think it is a good idea to go messing around looking for grenades. I can't believe I even have to say that sentence out loud; seriously, did you hear how terrible that sounded? Besides, it is Sam's wedding week."

"Which is again why it is so important to find them." Gladys crossed her arms and put on her best schoolteacher-end-of-discussion face. "What if the arms dealers deliver them in the middle of the ceremony?"

Before I could point out the absurdity of that statement by reminding her that she had chosen to give the bakery address, of all things, the swinging door between the kitchen and the café opened.

"Umm, guys." Victoria spoke softly, white as a sheet. "There's someone here to see Gladys."

"Can it wait?" Sam asked.

Victoria swallowed and shook her head side to side. "No, I don't think it can. And you two may want to come also." She jerked her head toward the café and disappeared back through the door, leaving it swinging in her wake.

"We are not finished," I pointed a finger at Gladys.

She patted my hand. "I know, we still have a lot to do to find those arms dealers and get rid of those smoke bombs."

And out she strolled.

"She has to be the most stubborn woman in the universe." I crossed my arms.

Sam laughed. "You're just jealous that she is the only person who can beat you at that particular trait."

"Bite me. Come on, let's go find out what is such a big deal out front." I led the way out front and wished for the life of me that I imagined the scene that greeted us.

"What's this? Another one?" A large bald man waved an equally large gun around the room. "Get over there with the others. I only have business with the old lady."

Quick as lightning, I pushed Sam back behind the kitchen door before she was noticed. Under the cover of Gladys's outraged protests of the 'old lady' comment, I hastily whispered to Sam. "Call the cops or somebody. And stay back."

Moving almost as fast as my heart was racing, I crossed from behind the counter and joined BeeBee, Eva, and Victoria at a small table.

Listening closely, I tried to catch up to the conversation.

Gun Guy clearly grew tired of Gladys's complaints. "Quiet!" he shouted, taking a menacing step closer to her.

Gladys eyed the gun. Her hand fisted.

Dear God, I prayed, *don't let Gladys try something that should only be done in movies.* Thankfully, my prayer was heard. Gladys relaxed her fist then crossed her arms.

"Now, I told you the money is due Friday. You have two days." He held up a hand when Gladys opened her mouth, undoubtedly to argue some more.

"Money? What money?" The words came out in a rush and I earned my own cutting glare from Gun Guy for interrupting. "Sorry," I shrugged. "Late to the party and all. Maybe we can give you the money now. What money does she owe?" I stalled, hoping to buy time for Sam to get somebody on the phone and to the bakery. *What could be taking so long?*

"Money for goods ordered." He gestured the gun at the counter, making me cringe again. "You want to break open that little register and tell me there's $500 cash in it?"

Gladys stomped. "I already told you, I didn't receive the smoke bombs and I'm not paying for them until I get them."

Gun Guy growled, actually growled, a deep feral sound. I got the impression he wasn't used to not getting his way. As a whole, our little group had that effect on people.

Rising, careful not to let the tremor in my legs show, I moved toward the counter. "Why don't I just check? I think there is probably a few hundred dollars. We could give you what we have and call it good, since the ordered items never arrived." I almost made it to the counter. Almost home-free for the little panic button that Griff had insisted on installing not long ago.

"Don't even think about it, girly. Get away from that counter and anything back there." Gun Guy was obviously smarter than he looked. "Keep your dollars. Get the $500 and be ready for my call." He slammed a cell phone onto the nearest table and backed out of the room.

7

Chapter 7

Officer Jack arrived a scant eight minutes after our newfound friend left. Disappointment flared inside of me that it had been such a close miss but I dared not comment on the response time.

Sam had explained that dispatch took their sweet time asking about the nature of the emergency, and since Sam had no way of knowing what was happening without revealing herself, it had been hard to convince them that she wasn't some prank caller.

"Sorry about the delay," Officer Jack scratched his ear with his pencil, just above his bad sideburns. "Bad wreck out near the highway. Had to wait for a junior deputy to arrive to work the scene because we're short-staffed this week. So, what can you tell me about this guy?"

The four of us took turns describing Gun Guy. It seemed, besides the gun and the shiny cue-ball head of course, that we all noticed a little something different: a scar above his left elbow, a barbell tattoo peaking over the neckline of his t-shirt, whoppingly ginormous feet.

"Rude." Gladys counted on her fingers the things she had noticed when her turn came. "Mean. Been hit with the ugly stick. Big."

I squeezed Sam's arm as I held in my laughter. I wondered how the sketch artist would go about illustrating those particular characteristics.

How Officer Jack even kept a straight face when he thanked Gladys for her observations, I didn't have a clue, but somehow, he did.

Officer Jack turned his attention to Sam. "And you?"

"I didn't see him. I only called 911."

"That's everybody then?" He searched our faces. With our nods and affirmatives, Officer Jack took his leave. "Call me if you think of anything else."

The bell over the door had barely finished jingling for his exit when the same noise announced the door opening again.

"Samantha!" Landon reached Sam in three strides. "Are you okay? I saw the cop car outside?"

"I'm fine."

Crossing my arms, I pursed my lips and assumed my best offended posture. "Why do you assume the worst? Why do the cops have to be here because something is wrong? What if they simply woke up today craving a raspberry-jam and almond sliver thumbprint cookie instead of a jelly donut?"

Sam snickered.

"Okay smarty pants, tell me: what did the nice police officer order?"

I slumped. "Nothing."

A smarmy grin leapt to Landon's face before he remembered he should be worried instead of triumphant. The grin transformed quickly into a deep frown. "What happened?"

The bell jingled again.

This time, I let out a deep sigh. "Not you, too?" Small towns were wonderful. Until they weren't. Can't even get questioned by the cops without your boyfriend knowing in less than ten minutes. I'd bet money that Flo called him from her flower shop next door.

Griff came over and wrapped me in his arms. Talking above my head, he asked Landon, "So, did they confess to whatever nefarious nonsense they've gotten mixed up in this time?"

"Nope, you're right on time. They were just about to explain." Landon pulled out a chair for Sam and for BeeBee who was closest to them.

The rest of us took seats of our own. Gladys harumphed and complained about time being wasted, but sat as well.

"Who wants to start?" Griff asked, eyeing each one of us in turn.

Seeing Gladys lean forward to talk, I launched into a quick explanation before she could tell the guys more than was good for us. Namely, I skirted around the fact that this accidental purchase had been intended for the bachelorette party. If they found that out, Sam and I would have permanent shadows until the wedding.

After I finished, Landon asked the next logical question, if you could find logic anywhere in this scenario. "Where does this guy want you to bring the payment that you owe for the smoke bombs?"

I might have also left eased around the word grenades. Sam and I had given Gladys enough grief on the subject already.

"A pier on the beach," Gladys answered nonchalantly.

Sam lifted a brow at me and I gave a tiny, swift shake of my head. I hadn't been in the room yet for that part of the exchange, so I didn't know the exact location.

Griff shifted, clearly preparing to ask more questions, when the front door bell jingled yet again. Saved by customers.

"Well, we have to get back to work." I stood, kissing Griff on the cheek as I did. "Stop by after work to sample some desserts that we're going to be trying out for the wedding reception."

Pulling me closer, Griff whispered in my ear. "I feel like there's more you aren't telling me."

"Of course, but only for my own good." I winked and hurried to the counter to check our stock of goodies while Victoria took the customer's order. A small line of people continued to trickle in the door.

Landon gave Sam a soft kiss goodbye and left behind Griff.

8

Chapter 8

"Let's go over what we've made so far."

BeeBee nodded to me and began walking around the room pointing out our wedding samples. "White chocolate puppy chow, white chocolate macadamia blondies, white chocolate almond truffles, and white chocolate mousse. The white chocolate bread pudding is in the oven."

"And I'm almost done prepping the white chocolate lasagna," Victoria added.

Sam and Gladys were working the café out front. I insisted on keeping most of the menu a surprise from Sam until it was time to taste and she was being a good sport about it. Eva volunteered to bus tables so the other two girls could help me in the kitchen. It was surreal to think how only a year or so ago, Sam and I were running the bakery and café all on our own. Having a team of people was a huge help, and being able to count them all as friends, well, that was a blessing that I definitely didn't take for granted.

BeeBee joined Victoria at the stainless-steel work island. Peering suspiciously into the pan, she said, "Explain to me about the lasagna again. It's still a dessert, right? Does it involve pasta? That seems weird."

Victoria and I laughed. I let Victoria run with the explanation as I consulted my list, checking things off and making notes.

"No pasta involved. It is pure dessert and I can't wait to taste it. There is a golden cookie crumb crust, a layer of cream cheese, white chocolate pudding, and tiny white chocolate curls atop a layer of whipped cream." Victoria pointed to a bar of chocolate. "You can go ahead and start making the curls if you want."

BeeBee shaved a large pile of white chocolate curls. She sprinkled them liberally over the lasagna when Victoria finished smoothing the whipped cream into one silky layer. "I guess we don't bake it like normal lasagna then?"

"Nope, just pop it in the fridge for a bit."

"What's left on today's list?" BeeBee asked.

"Hmm?" As sometimes happens, checking over one list had led to me making another, and another. With effort, I drug my gaze away from my notepad. I had a thing for lists. If list making were a superpower, it would be mine. "What's that?"

"Welcome back. I said, what else do we need to make for today's samples?"

I dropped my pen back into my apron pocket and flipped back to my original list, hoping the girls didn't realize I'd been making a list of things to do to either pay off the arms dealers or help the police find them. "I think that's it for today. I'll work up some mini wedding cake samples at my apartment tonight and bring them for Sam and Landon to try tomorrow."

"Tomorrow?" Victoria cocked her head. "Isn't tomorrow the day y'all are going to try on dresses and to get Sam's wedding dress?"

"Shoot!" I slapped a hand across my forehead. What a thing to forget! "Yes, you're right. Okay, then. I'll bring samples here for Landon to stop and try. Sam's samples will just go with us for taste-testing along the way."

Victoria nodded, satisfied.

The café/kitchen door swung open. Sam, Gladys and Eva entered, followed by Griff and Landon.

"Everything is all locked up," Sam said.

"Where's the grub?" Griff asked taking my hand.

"Patience," I smiled. Whisking away the last of the dirty dishes and empty trays, I gestured to the stools around the work table. "Everyone, take a seat."

BeeBee passed out plates and napkins while Victoria helped me serve the dessert samples.

"These look wonderful!" Sam exclaimed.

I shrugged. "Don't be too impressed, they aren't decorated yet. Today is only about taste. We can focus on appearance on the actual day."

Everyone agreed that the desserts were delicious.

"No need to change a thing," Sam declared.

As a group, we made quick work of the cleanup then all headed out separately to go home for the night. Griff stayed with me as I locked up.

"This is going to be one of those times you don't let me keep my secrets, isn't it?" I asked as we walked beneath the light pole to our vehicles.

"Not when your secret is likely to jeopardize your safety." Griff crossed his arms and leaned against my truck. "So, what did you leave out of the story? Clearly, the man in the bakery was pretty threatening for the cops to be called."

I blew out a puff of air. "Gladys may or may not have managed to online order those smoke bombs we told you about from a group of arms dealers."

Griff waited. I swear the man could get information out of a mute if he wanted to. I continued. There was no way I was about to start lying to him and he'd likely find out eventually. "The man who was shot in front of the bakery, he was also connected to the arms dealers. A delivery boy of sorts. He had Gladys's name and this address. Now, the arms dealers want to be paid."

"How do y'all even manage?"

Leaning my head against his chest, I sighed. "At least it actually wasn't my fault this time."

"But you still managed to find a dead body." A muscle in Griff's jaw ticked. Clearly, he wasn't happy. Well, that made two of us.

"Technically, I found him alive. Then he died. But yeah, not my favorite part either way."

9

Chapter 9

The next morning, I loaded up my cake samples and drove to the Ooey Gooey Goodness Bakery. Believe it or not, I'd slept a lot better after telling Griff everything that was really going on. I'd also had an idea.

I called Gladys on the way to the bakery and asked her to meet me and Sam there.

She agreed readily, especially when I confirmed the wedding cake samples would also be there.

"Morning!" I called out as I nudged the back door to the bakery kitchen open wider with my foot. Juggling three Tupperware containers, my keys, and purse, I made it inside I shouldered the door shut behind me.

BeeBee hurried over. "Let me help you."

"Thanks," I whooshed. "I don't think that top container was going to make it much longer."

"No sacrificing the desserts. This is wedding cake we are talking about; that would have to be a bad sign if it fell on the floor, right?"

I laughed. "Oh, come on, BeeBee. I don't believe in signs and omens."

"Still," Victoria moved closer, lifting the lid to inhale the sugary aroma from one container. "Wedding cake is kind of sacred. Even if it is just samples. And these particular samples smell delicious. Dropping it would have been a tragedy for sure."

As Victoria shut the lid, Gladys bustled in the back door. "Don't tell me y'all are in here sampling things without me. You know I'm the official Ooey Gooey Goodness Bakery taste-tester. I take that job very seriously."

Laying a hand on her shoulder, I gave a reassuring squeeze. "Not a bit of tasting without you. Or the bride, of course."

"Bride-schmide," Gladys winked. "I don't know why we have to wait on her."

Hearing the key in the lock once more, I turned to greet Sam as she entered. "Speak of the devil."

"Someone was talking about my mother?" she asked innocently, earning a laugh.

"No, you." Gladys pulled her inside. "Piper says we can't try *your* wedding cake samples without *you* for some ridiculous reason."

"Should we wait for Eva, too?" Sam asked, always politeness itself.

BeeBee shook her head. "I told her to sleep in today and come by later."

"In that case," Sam clapped her hands together. "By all means, let's get tasting!"

I passed out the samples, leaving one container full. "This is Landon's sample batch," I showed Victoria and BeeBee. They nodded.

I described each sample as we tasted them: white amaretto cake with white chocolate ganache, white chocolate and raspberry layer cake with white chocolate buttercream, and a dark chocolate fudge cake with a white chocolate ganache.

Half an hour later, we had sampled everything twice and Sam had decided on her favorite flavor. "I definitely want this white chocolate and raspberry," she said. "It's light and fluffy but packed with so much flavor!"

"Okay, okay," Victoria made shooing motions with her hands. "Y'all need to get moving so you can go try on wedding dresses while BeeBee and I catch up on this morning's baking before customers start beating down the door."

"Sounds like a plan." Grabbing all three of our purses from the hook by the door, I ushered Gladys and Sam outside.

Sam's delicately thin eyebrow arched. "Not to be a spoil-sport, but no wedding dress shop is open at this time of morning. Nothing is open this time of morning; well, besides us, of course."

"I know. But we aren't just wedding dress shopping today."

"We're not?"

Gladys shimmied. "I knew it! I knew it when you called and invited me to tag along today. You have a plan for the arms dealers, don't you?"

"I have the sketchy beginnings of a plan. First, we need more information from you. Where did Gun Guy – did anyone catch his name, by the way? No? Okay. Where did Gun Guy want you to bring the money?"

"Let's see. He called it Pirate Pier."

I groaned. "That's what I was afraid of."

"Is it far away?" Gladys asked.

"Not far enough, in my opinion." I unlocked my truck. "Come on, I'll drive and explain on the way."

10

Chapter 10

After reminding Gladys that Pirate Pier was on the beach near where I'd almost been murdered, I ran through the details of my plan.

"Piper, you know you're my best friend and everything, but how in the world do you classify that as a plan?" Sam crossed her arms. "We're just going to waltz out to Pirate Pier, the most notoriously criminal infested hang-out with the most noticeably absent law enforcement presence, and see if anyone knows where highly dangerous arms dealers are staying?"

"Come on, we've had worse plans."

She snorted. "You must mean the one where we ended up tied up in a massage parlor and thinking we were going to be killed? Sure."

"See! What's the likelihood of something like that happening again?"

I drove past the turnoff that would take us to the beach closest to Pirate Pier. There wasn't a sign or anything, but I'd lived here forever and I knew where it was. So did Sam.

"Hey! I thought we were going to scope out the pier?"

I nod. "We are. That doesn't mean we have to park my truck where anybody we make mad can see what I drive."

"Why do you assume we're going to make someone mad?" Gladys asked.

I ignored that and pulled my truck into a gas station parking lot that backed up to a small trailhead leading over the dunes to the beach. "Okay. We can walk from here and look like we're just strolling down the beach."

Gladys paused beside the truck. "What do we do if we don't find the arms dealers?"

Throwing her arms in the air, Sam said, "I think the better question is what do we do if we manage to find them? Do you plan to pay them?"

"Of course not!" Gladys scoffed.

"I've been thinking about that." I tapped my foot. Would my idea work? I didn't know. I did think we might as well try. "Here's the plan."

Minutes later, our feet hit the sand. Slipping off my shoes, I briefly prayed I wouldn't need them for running away from anyone or anything.

Within ten minutes, Pirate Pier was visible.

"Okay, I'll go first and you two can wait over there by the water."

"Are you sure we should let her go alone?" Sam asked as we watched Gladys slogging through the sand toward the support columns below the pier.

"No, not really, but at least this way we'll have a head start if we need to call for help or go get the truck."

Gladys had just stepped into the shadow of the pier when a lanky boy appeared from behind the second column. He stayed in the shadows. From where we stood, I couldn't make out any distinguishing features.

"This is excruciating," Sam muttered.

"Are you biting your nails?" I slapped her hands down. "Your wedding is this weekend, don't go messing up that manicure."

Sooner than expected, Gladys turned and walked back to us.

"Well? How'd it go?"

Gladys linked arms with us and kept moving. "Fine for now. Let's keep moving just in case." She grunted. "This darned sand is hard to walk on in sandals."

Once off the beach, Gladys rehashed her conversation with the teen.

"He's a lookout. I told him I wanted to find the big bald ugly guy slinging guns. Said that I needed to tell him that Friday payment won't work for me because I'll be at a rehearsal dinner with three or four people in a secluded house on the beach with no time to come all the way back here."

"Did he tell you where to find the arms dealers? Or even just the bald guy?" I asked.

"Nope. The kid said he'd rather shoot himself in the foot than give up information like that. He did say that he would give my message to the *big dogs* but that they weren't going to be happy about it."

"A secluded house with three or four people?" Sam shook her head in disbelief as she opened the door of the truck. "You laid it on a little thick don't you think?"

"Maybe. Maybe not." Gladys buckled her seat belt. "I guess we will just see if anyone shows up to collect the cash from me at the rehearsal dinner."

Pulling onto the highway, I headed back toward downtown. "If they show up, they'll probably be there to do more than collect cash. Time for phase two of this plan."

11

Chapter 11

Officer Jack looked less than pleased to see us being escorted to his desk.

His mood soured even further when we told him why we were there.

"You did what?!?"

I cringed. "Set a trap," I repeated. "Or it will be a trap, anyway, if you send a few officers to Sam's rehearsal dinner tomorrow night out on Blue Beach Way."

"Of all the crazy things I've heard in my years, three women setting themselves up as bait for arms dealers is one of the looniest."

"Will you help?" Sam asked.

Officer Jack sighed. "Don't see that I have much choice at this point. What time is this dinner thing?"

I left the meeting with Officer Jack feeling relieved and a little bit excited. By tomorrow, we could get Gladys out of this sticky situation and potentially help catch a lot of dangerous people. I sent a quick prayer that everything worked as planned and then pushed all thoughts of arms dealers and murderers aside. Time to focus on Sam.

12

Chapter 12

"There are so many to choose from!"

Standing in the middle of Bridal Belle's, a bridal store bigger than I'd ever imagined and had no idea existed so close to our little town, I raked my fingers through my hair. "Sam, are you telling me you don't even have choices for your wedding dress narrowed down yet?"

"I thought I did. But they all look so much more beautiful in the store than online." Sam put on her best pouty face. "Help me try them on? Then I can get an idea of twice as many in half the time."

"Are you kidding?" I yelped loud enough to make the bridal concierge frown at us from her desk. Lowering my voice, I said, "You can't actually think seeing me in a dress will help you decide if you like it?"

"Pretty please with a chocolate bar on top?"

"Fine," I grumbled. "But note that I'm doing this under protest."

"Noted," Gladys and Sam replied simultaneously.

A short while later, we stood in front of the dressing room, arms loaded down with gowns that Sam insisted she had to see.

An assistant joined us. "Ladies, are you ready to try some things on?"

"All of these." Sam held out an armful of dresses then nodded in my direction. "And all of those."

"Oh my!"

Gladys settled into a high-backed chair.

"Well then, let's begin." The assistant hung our monstrous pile of dresses in an extra-large fitting room with a folded-up privacy screen. "For bridal parties," she explained.

"Do you care which one I start with?" I asked Sam, taking off my shoes and socks.

She raised her palms. "Whichever you want. We'll see them all regardless."

Letting out a longsuffering sigh, I pulled the privacy screen shut between us.

I sorted through the dresses Sam needed me to model for her. Too fluffy. Too lacy. Too long. I didn't know what my friend was thinking with some of these. There seemed to be one dress for every conceivable style on this rack.

At last, I knew I had to just dive in. Unfortunately, my first dive had me drowning in layers of fabric, most of which I didn't even know the name of. Lace, satin, who knows. "Umm, a little help in here!"

Sam opened the screen up and after a few tugs, I had on the first dress. "This is terrible," I scowled. Just for good measure, I tossed a handful of the full skirt around. If someone wanted to dress up as a giant bell for their wedding, this was the dress. Sam, I noticed, looked perfectly comfortable in a ball gown style dress with a beaded corset.

"Hey! I'm out here, you know." Gladys called loudly enough to make us each wince. "I can't see through walls."

"Here we come," Sam spoke softly through the door.

Gladys clapped and whistled, earning a few tight-lipped frowns from the assistant.

"You know," I told the poor woman, "we probably can help each other with zippers and all that stuff. How about we let you know when our lovely bride has made a final decision?"

With a curt nod, she scurried over to a young bride and presumably her mother that had just entered.

"Next," Gladys shooed us toward the dressing room.

As we tried on dress after dress, Sam and I carried on a broken conversation between trips in and out to show Gladys the dresses.

Toward the end, I brought up the guilt I'd been feeling all day. "I should've asked you about setting up the arms dealers using your rehearsal." I kicked the hem of my dress out of the way. "Sorry about that."

"No worries. I'd rather get that whole mess over with before the wedding anyway." She twirled, looking stunning yet again. "Now come on, let's show Gladys."

Upon exiting the dressing room after dress number four, we found Gladys eating a small bag of popcorn. Popcorn! I looked twice. Yep, still popcorn.

"Gladys, where in the world did you get popcorn," I whispered. I glanced around, highly doubting that popcorn among all of these expensive gowns would be allowed.

"In my purse, obviously. What, do you think I go around with food stuck in my bra?" She rolled her eyes as if I was the crazy one. "And it's kettle corn. Already popped and flavored. Easy to transport."

I smacked a hand over my face. Denial. Denial felt like a good choice.

Turning, I rushed back into the dressing room.

"We better hurry up with these last dresses before Gladys gets caught," I said.

Sam unzipped me. "You're probably right. I only have two left. How about you?"

"I think I'm done." I shifted hangers around. "Oh. No, one more for me. I must have missed it."

Sam declared one of the dresses a no without even leaving the dressing room. That left us one apiece. "Here we come," she peeked around the doorframe at Gladys. Last ones."

As we turned and spun for Gladys, she simply stared.

"Both of them!" Gladys gave a thumbs up. "Seriously, I love them. Buy them both."

I laughed. "She doesn't need two wedding dresses."

Sam pulled me over to the mirror with her and studied both dresses. "They are fabulous," she murmured.

"You have to choose," I said. "Which one do you want to see in all of your wedding pictures?"

"This one," she smiled softly, fingering the delicate patterns, filigree they informed me later, reminiscent of waves covering the snug bodice. The dress sucked in at her thighs and then flared out in an entirely different material creating layers of delicate flounces to just a hair above the floor. Frothy. That described it perfectly. The dress frothed around Sam's ankles just as so many tiny bubbles frothed along the water's edge as the tide washed in and out. A gorgeous beach dress for a gorgeous bride. My heart filled with joy for my friend. Her big day was finally almost here and it felt so strange yet so right. She deserved a wonderful marriage and someone to cherish her for the amazing woman she was.

"Perfect." I hugged her. "You do look perfect." I asked Gladys to find the assistant while we changed out of the gowns but she was still eating the kettle corn. "Never mind. I'll go. This dress thankfully won't take long to get out of. It is much simpler than those other concoctions."

Sam nudged me. "Maybe you should take Gladys to the truck while I pay, in case she has any more goodies in her purse."

"Smart idea."

"Where now?" Gladys asked as soon as Sam joined us in the truck.

I shrugged. "I hadn't planned anything past wedding dresses. You?"

Sam checked her watch. "It's past lunch. Let's find food. We can call the girls and check in when we finish."

13

Chapter 13

A giant yawn escaped me. I'd like to say that Friday dawned bright and clear, but truly I had no idea. I'd arrived at the bakery well before dawn and was feeling every one of those missed minutes of sleep.

Satisfied with my frosting crumb coat, I carefully placed the beginning of Sam's wedding cake into the freezer. Now, to get started on the decorations.

The back door opened. "Morning!" Victoria said.

Before the door closed, I glimpsed a still gray sky. I checked my watch. "You're awfully early."

"Regardless of the fact that you are a one-woman dessert machine,

I thought I'd come lend a hand anyway. There's so much to do." She donned an apron. "Put me to work on whatever you want to do least."

She'd barely finished her sentence when in walked BeeBee and Eva.

"Let me guess," I wagged my head back and forth. "Y'all just couldn't stay away from a little extra work either."

BeeBee winked. "Extra work is our favorite." She rubbed her hands together. "Let's make wedding dessert masterpieces."

My drowsiness faded to the background. Having such incredible people always willing to go above and beyond was invigorating and their bubbling excitement was contagious. We'd done plenty of the regular baking prep work the evening before, after Sam, Gladys, and I returned from lunch and dress shopping. Sam, for once in her life, hadn't made me buy a new dress saying the wedding was beachy casual and I decided to count my good fortune instead of arguing.

Thinking back on yesterday continued to boost my mood. I shook off the reverie and focused. "Okay, Eva, you can roll truffles and BeeBee, you dip them into the coating chocolate." I pointed out their station and the girls set to work. "Victoria, here is the recipe for the white chocolate buttercream that I need made for the wedding cake. If you will work on a big batch of it, then I'll start putting together the decorations for everything."

"You got it."

In no time, all of the regular desserts were finished. I only needed to frost and decorate the cake now. "Break time," I called to the girls. From the refrigerator, I pulled out several bottles of water and handed them around. "Everything looks incredible. I couldn't have done it without you three. After we box these up, I'll help you with the rest of today's regular baking and then work on the cake after the café opens.""

Victoria surveyed everything. "I have platters and serving trays to use for setting up. Are we closing early today or is Gladys coming in to cover a shift?"

"Closing early."

The remaining morning passed swiftly. Griff stopped by with lunch and I showed him Sam's cake.

"Wow! She's really going to love it."

I closed the freezer door back. "Thanks, I hope so."

We opened up the bags of food at the work table in the center of the kitchen.

"This is delicious," I told Griff as I munched casually on some fried shrimp.

He studied me. "Okay. What's up? Something is on your mind."

So much for casual. I swallowed, licking my lips which suddenly felt dry. "Well, there's this teensy little thing I forgot to tell you about."

"Uh-huh?" Griff put down his ribs and leaned back, one arm resting on the work table.

I shifted uncomfortably under his stare. "We may have unofficially invited the arms dealers or their thugs to the rehearsal dinner tonight."

I watched as Griff's jaw clenched. I swear the man was counting to ten before he answered me. I rushed on before he could get there. "Don't worry, we enlisted Officer Jack's help."

"Explain," he said through gritted teeth.

I doubted the full explanation would make him any happier but I gave it to him anyway.

Griff bent his head into both hands. Seconds went by. Finally, he scrubbed both hands across his face and sighed, sitting back up. "What in the world were you thinking?"

"That somebody needed to get these creeps off of Gladys's back." I pursed my lips. Maybe it was a harebrained scheme. And maybe we should have gotten cops involved at the beginning instead of the end of the plan. Still, Griff new I would do anything for my friends. We'd been down this road before.

"You don't always have to save the day, Piper." Griff balled up the rest of his food and tossed it in a trash can. "And it would be nice if you would start thinking of yourself instead of everyone else first. Maybe even, I don't know, ask for help!"

"But..."

"No buts. You're going to get yourself hurt or killed. Or don't you even care?" Griff's frustration rolled off of him in waves. "I've got to get back to work."

And then he was gone.

My heart stuttered. My little world was rocked. I don't think I'd ever made him quite that angry before. I pulled my phone from my apron pocket and clicked on messages but hesitated. Should I call instead? Should I just give him some time? Time! I jumped up. "Shoot," I muttered to myself. "I'm going to be late."

Ten minutes later, I whipped my truck into a parking spot at the nail salon. Part of the bachelorette festivities included mani-pedis. After that, the hair salon.

14

Chapter 14

R egardless of our relaxing afternoon, my anxiety crept higher as we milled around on the beach waiting for the wedding rehearsal to begin.

Two plain-clothes police officers ambled back and forth among the wedding party. I hoped they looked like they fit in more to strangers than they looked to me.

"Is everyone ready?" Pastor Dan asked.

Landon and Griff moved into their spots. I took my place behind Victoria, who was standing in for the bride tonight. Sam had a front row seat to watch everything and couldn't stop smiling up at Landon.

I gripped my seashell bouquet so tightly that my fingers ached as I walked down the aisle marked off by glass starfish. Our trap was laid but the waiting was worse than I'd imagined. No scary men materialized down the beach. My eyes bounced back and forth, from the pastor to the beach to the ocean and back, as he spoke the words that he would say tomorrow. No gun-toting maniacs appeared. I expected to feel relieved; instead, the heaviness in my chest increased. *Were the bad guys not coming after all?*

The rehearsal sped by thanks to the simplicity of the wedding. Sam and Landon were only having Griff and I stand up with them. No flower girl. No ring bearer. Victoria would handle hitting play on a digital playlist for the music. In a matter of minutes, everyone was satisfied with practice.

"Who's ready to eat?" Gladys asked.

Cheers sounded and we all made our way to the beach house.

My overactive imagination wouldn't let up. I found myself eyeing the space below the steps, the trunks of the thick palm trees by the deck, the shadows between everyone's cars. I gave myself a mental shake. Time to celebrate Sam and Landon, to enjoy this time and let the professionals do their jobs.

Without fail, good food and good friends did the trick. Hours passed and I relaxed my guard, the tension eased. I came to accept the fact that our trap hadn't panned out.

"Good night!" I hugged BeeBee and Eva as they headed home for the night.

BeeBee tried one more time to help. "Are you sure we can't stay to clean up?"

"Positive," Sam said, overhearing as she came to tell the girls bye. "It's just a matter of popping food in the fridge and wiping up some crumbs."

"That's right. Everything else we can just leave decorated until tomorrow." I gave them a nudge toward the door. "Get some rest."

Pastor Dan and his wife had gone home well before dark. Victoria left to help her aunt with some things not long after. With BeeBee and Eva departing, that left only the officers, Gladys, Griff and myself. I noticed Sam and Landon looked tired.

Gladys must have seen them stifling yawns as well. "I'm out of here. You kids kept me up past my bedtime," she joked.

With Gladys gone, I dismissed the two plain-clothes police officers. They'd stayed far longer than I expected already.

"Let me walk you to your truck," Griff said, taking my hand.

He squeezed it extra tight and seemed to be moving a bit stiff. I wondered if he was still angry with me.

Sam blew us both a kiss and ushered us out the door onto the deck. Looking forward to my comfy bed, I went directly toward the stairs that led to our cars but Griff tugged me to the opposite end of the deck. The end facing the beach. *Uh-oh*, I thought. If Griff wanted to talk that could be good or bad.

"Piper," Griff stared straight into my eyes. His hand squeezed mine again. "You are one of the most frustrating people I've ever met."

My stomach twisted. I guess I had my answer. Griff wanting to talk was going to be bad. Stiffening, I waited to hear the rest.

"I've never met anyone as stubborn as you. You're headstrong; you never listen to reason. Goodness knows you never ask for help."

I shifted back and pulled my hand from his. "Now wait one second."

Griff gently placed a finger on my lips. "I'm not finished."

I restrained myself from biting his finger to show him how I felt about being shushed, but it was a close call.

"As I was saying," Griff dropped to one knee. "I've never met a soul like you. And I definitely don't want to lose you before you're even mine. Piper Rivers, will you marry me?"

I blinked. And stared. My boyfriend held up a beautiful ring, small sparkling diamonds arranged in a heart shape with an arrow piercing through it, one little ruby in the arrowhead and one in the fletching.

Tears sprang to my eyes as I nodded.

Griff stood. He held the ring poised over my finger and I think I forgot to breathe. "Is that a yes?" he asked in a low voice.

"Yes!"

Slipping the delicate ring onto my hand, Griff lifted me and spun in a circle. "She said yes!" he hollered.

Suddenly, laughter, whoops, hollers, and clapping surrounded us. Our friends started appearing from the woodwork, literally. BeeBee and Eva emerged from around the corner of the deck. Sam and Landon popped out of the house, where they had very clearly been listening near the door. Even Gladys waved from behind a post at the bottom of the stairs.

"You all knew about this?"

Sam hugged me. "Of course!"

"I even baked your wedding cake," Gladys said proudly.

"My wedding cake?"

Griff grimaced. "I hadn't gotten to that part yet."

"Oops." Gladys lifted her hands in a *how was I supposed to know* shrug.

"How do you feel about a double wedding?" Griff asked.

"A double wedding? Are you kidding me? As in, tomorrow?"

"You said yes," Griff winked and pulled me tight against his warm chest. "I don't plan to give you time to change your mind."

I leaned back to look in his eyes. They were serious. "What about my parents?"

"Already on their way," he assured me. "A delay at the airport is the only reason they weren't here to congratulate us with everyone else."

"I don't have a dress."

Sam wagged a finger. "Uh-uh-uh. You have a dress. You may not realize it yet, but it is your favorite one from our shopping trip today."

"I guess if I bring up anything else, you'll tell me it is taken care of, too?"

"That about sums it up." Griff's laugh lines crinkled around his eyes.

"So basically, we're getting married tomorrow and that is the end of that?" I clarified. I slapped his chest playfully. "And you called me headstrong."

Gravel crunched on the other side of the house and a car engine hummed.

"Hey! Did you hear someone pull up? Maybe it's my parents."

Gladys held a hand out for me to stay put. "I'll bring them around back. You just stay right here and enjoy your moment. By the way, dark chocolate."

"What about dark chocolate?"

"The flavor of your wedding cake," she laughed over her shoulder as she rounded the corner, her head shaking with mirth as she walked.

"Y'all are amazing!" I couldn't wrap my head around all of this. "I can't believe I'm getting shanghaied into a wedding. How in the world did y'all pull this off so fast?"

Caught up in all of the excitement, I didn't realize right away that the noises coming from the driveway weren't greetings, or the voices of my parents, until Landon's face took on a puzzled frown. I quieted and the noises became clearer. Arguing.

"Stay here," Landon told Sam. Before he'd gone two feet, gunshots rang out.

Gladys screamed.

My heart stopped. Griff and Landon leaped over the deck railing. I hurtled headlong down the stairs and around the corner. Pounding through the sand and then gravel, my blood ran cold when I saw the sight before me.

I heard Sam's sharp gasp before she clenched my hand. Together, we stumbled the rest of the way forward to where Gladys lay sprawled beside her car. Griff leaned over her, checking her pulse. Landon came sprinting back from the road.

"I lost him," he said. "Is she okay?"

Griff nodded. "Gunshot in the thigh and a bump on the head. Unconscious, but breathing strong. Call 911."

Sam dialed, her fingers moving like lightning across the screen of her phone.

A sob escaped my throat. "Who? Who did this?" I asked, fearing I knew the answer.

"A big bald guy with a gun almost as big as him." Landon raked his hand through his hair.

My stomach turned. Nausea flooded through me. My fault. This was my fault.

Griff removed his belt and tied a makeshift tourniquet around Gladys's thigh.

15

Chapter 15

"Where have you two been?" From her propped-up position in the hospital bed, it appeared Gladys had requested every extra pillow on this floor level. She scowled at us. "Now, one of you help me get dressed while the other of you goes and signs some release forms. We have a wedding to get to."

Sam twirled a piece of hair around her finger and bit her lip.

I tried ignoring the request. "How are you feeling? Can we get you some coffee?"

Gladys narrowed her eyes. "You can get me the heck out of here; I think I just said that."

"No can do." I moved to one side of the bed and Sam sat down on the other. "The doctor says one more day."

"Fiddlesticks."

"We want you to do what he says," Sam said. "Please. For our peace of mind."

"I am not staying in this hospital. We have a bachelorette party to finish and two weddings to get to." Gladys reached for the call button on the side of the bed.

Sam grabbed Gladys's hand at the same time that I covered the button. "We are not having any wedding if you leave this hospital," I threatened. Only the widening of Sam's eyes made me realize I'd jumped in and spoken for her also. Ooops. Well, I already basically ruined her rehearsal night, surely, she could forgive me for delaying her wedding, too. I winced. At least, I hoped so.

Gladys shook off Sam's hand and frowned. She couldn't quite hide the wince of pain when she shifted in the bed though. The doctor was right, she definitely needed to stay here and rest.

"You are not postponing the wedding. Either of them. Not after how long it took those two men to get around to proposing." Gladys tapped her fingers on the bedsheet.

"What are you plotting now?" Sam asked.

"I'll make you a deal," Gladys said.

I raised my eyebrows. So now we were negotiating?

"What kind of deal?" Sam didn't look any more reassured by this prospect than I felt.

"You say if I leave, you'll postpone the weddings. Well, I say if I stay that you have to go through with the weddings as planned. Today. Otherwise, I'll just check myself out and go on home." She smiled triumphantly and relaxed back into her mound of pillows, watching us.

"What?" Sam spluttered.

I couldn't believe she was turning my ultimatum around on me. Sneaky woman. "You know we don't want to get married without you there."

"You can set up one of those livestream thingamabobs. I'll watch it from right here." Her mouth remained set in a straight line.

"You're serious, aren't you?" I studied Gladys. She only nodded. "Give us a minute. Sam?" I beckoned her to follow me out into the hall. Griff and Landon were waiting.

We told the guys the gist of how things stood. After five- or six-minutes discussion, Sam and I relented. We went back in the room to tell Gladys the weddings would go on.

Chapter 16

I wished I had a crowbar for peeling my eyelids open. I dozed on and off for maybe two hours tops after Gladys was whisked to the hospital last night. A hum of conversation pierced my consciousness and I groaned, stretched, and prepared to face the day.

"Coffee." Sam croaked beside me.

Blinking, I scanned the room. Sam and I were smushed together on a long ottoman in the center of the hospital waiting room. Griff and Landon were across from us, sitting straight up in two chairs, heads propped against the wall in positions that I feared would result in aching necks later today.

I stood and stretched, popping my back and rolling my own neck to ease the tension. Near the nurse's station, I found the source of the conversation that had woken me.

"Officer Jack," I greeted. "What are you doing here?"

Rubbing a hand across a pencil stuck behind his ear, he said, "I came to check on your friend. I also thought y'all might like an update."

"Please!" I motioned him to follow me back to our little corner of the room where the guys were now awake. Sam had successfully scrounged up coffee and waters.

"We haven't heard anything on Gladys yet," I told the officer. "What happened with the shooter?"

"We didn't find him, but thanks to your friend here knocking out a taillight with a rock and getting the license plate number, we did find the car in a body shop this morning. A high-end body shop, surprisingly; one of the last places we checked."

Sam wrapped both hands around her coffee. "That's great news! And great job, Landon!"

"I should have caught the guy." Landon shuffled his feet.

"Nonsense," I said. "Gladys is fortunate you and Griff scared that guy off so quickly."

Sam agreed. "Thank you, officer, for all of your hard work and for taking time to come and update us. We really appreciate it."

Officer Jack tipped his head to us and left us to celebrate this small piece of good news.

"I can't believe it." I sat back down and gulped from my water bottle, only to jump right back up when I saw the doctor making a beeline for our group.

"Family of Gladys Hill?" he asked.

"All of us," I said.

He seemed to consider that for a moment but decided not to question it. "She is out of surgery and we were able to remove the bullet without any complications. She's fortunate it didn't do more damage."

"And her head?" Landon asked.

"A bit of a goose egg but there are no signs of concussion this morning."

"Can we see her?" I pleaded, shifting impatiently in spite of Griff's ministrations to relax me.

"You may see her. Only two at a time, however, and I feel the need to warn you that the anesthesia seems to be making her a bit cranky."

Sam snorted. "That isn't the anesthesia. That's just Gladys when she isn't getting her way."

"Ah." The doctor smiled. "The nurses did mention demands to leave and attend a wedding." Growing serious again, he said, "I'm sorry but I've had to decline. She really needs to stay in bed and off that leg and I'd feel better monitoring her vitals another day due to the head wound and her age."

I chuckled. "We'll do you a favor, doctor, and we won't mention the age comment to Gladys or she'll make her stay more uncomfortable for you than for her."

17

Chapter 17

"Pour me another glass, please."

Uncapping the bottle of sparkling rosé grape juice, non-alcoholic per hospital regulations, I filled Gladys's plastic goblet to the brim and handed it back.

"I'd like more of the red. Anyone else?" Sam poured her own drink and refilled Victoria's when she nodded.

Eva and I were having the sparkling white grape juice. BeeBee shared the rosé with Gladys, which to me tasted far too bitter and similar to actual wine.

Our impromptu bachelorette party was in full swing. Thanks to some well-placed boxes of chocolate, the nursing staff turned a blind eye to the two-visitor rule. We all squished into Gladys's room comfortably enough.

"What do you want to watch next?" Victoria manned the laptop that sat atop the wheeled bedside table. She rolled it closer to her and named off some chick-flick and a few action movies she had downloaded.

I flicked a few streamers out of my way, trying to see the options better. Yes, streamers. Gladys had sent us to her house to pick up my wedding cake. When we saw all of the decorations strewn across her living room, we couldn't let them go to waste. Sam had called the girls at the bakery and told them to close early while I loaded everything into the car.

Not long after lunch, and the aforementioned nurse-bribing, Gladys's hospital room was decked out in white and silver streamers, wedding ring balloons, regular white balloons, kissing-lip balloons, and a large banner that said *Sayonara to Single, Welcome to Wedded Bliss*.

Sam did put a stop to me using all of the confetti. Other than that, we'd brought in everything. It appeared Gladys had taken our requests to heart after the smoke grenade debacle because everything ended up pretty tame. Which was probably a good thing when you considered that the party was happening in a hospital room.

"Let's watch *Wedding Planner*," Sam said.

Digging around in the last box of party supplies, I held up a selection of facial cremes and masks. "Should we go ahead and put these on while we watch?"

"Definitely!"

"Yes."

"Sure!"

And so it was, that when the doctor made his rounds, he found a room full of teal-faced women eating popcorn, sipping sparkling juice, and generally having a fantastic time.

"What in blazes in going on in here?" he exclaimed, swatting a particularly thick clump of streamers away from his shoulder.

"Ooh-la-la, Piper! Did you order a doctor?"

I rolled my eyes and ignored Gladys. Turning to the doctor, I asked innocently, "Would you believe there's been research that says celebrations speed wound healing by fifty percent?"

"No." He clipped. "You have ten minutes to vacate this room. And take all this junk with you." His white coat flapped behind him as he spun on his heel and stalked out of the room.

"Sheesh," BeeBee laughed. "I feel sorry for the nurses if he figures out who let us in here."

With a brief nod, I clapped my hands. "You heard the man. Let's get this stuff packed up."

"I'll leave the laptop for you to watch the wedding on." Victoria walked Gladys through the finer points of how to connect to the video and wrote out some reminder instructions.

With a lot of hustle, we made our ten-minute deadline. I checked my watch as we exited the hospital. "Holy snickerdoodles! We spent the whole day in there?"

Sam yelped, giving my arm a squeeze. "Piper, we only have two hours to get ready for our weddings!"

18

Chapter 18

"Knock-knock."

"Come in," I called to my mom as Sam finished pinning a small comb into my hair. With a turquoise starfish and small pearls, it was the perfect beach hairpiece for my dark, shoulder-length hair.

"Girls!" Mom breathed. "You both look absolutely stunning."

Sam twirled. "Thank you."

"Thanks, Mom." I hugged her. "Sam gets all of the credit though. She tricked me into trying on dresses and then picked this one for me."

"It's fabulous."

I had to agree. The simple, fitted style hugged my body without being obscenely tight. Sleeveless, with a halter-top neckline and a cutout from my shoulder blades to my lower back, I'd never felt more beautiful.

"Shoes?" Mom asked.

"Barefoot." Sam and I shared a grin. Her mother would have been appalled; mine only nodded.

"Sand between your toes. I like it." She fluffed my hair and wiped a quick tear from her own eye before turning to Sam. "Samantha, dear, we thought, well." Mom hemmed and hawed, very unlike her.

"What is it?" I prodded. We didn't have much time before the wedding march.

Taking a deep breath, she clasped Sam's hands. "With your parents not present, we wondered if you would like to share a father-of-the-bride?"

Sam's eyes glistened and I was touched to see her pull my mom into a bear hug, or as close as one could get with all the frill around Sam's feet. "I'd like that very much."

A couple of minutes and a few more tears later, my Dad, with Sam on one side and me on the other, escorted us across the dunes and down the seashell-strewn aisle of sand to the veiled arbor on the shore where Pastor Dan, Landon, and Griff waited. My eyes strayed for one moment to the gorgeous orange and pink sunset reflecting on the ocean waves. Peace and calm settled over me, from my head to my toes. My heart filled with love and joy like I'd never known.

Perfection The moment crashed over me, silencing even the noise of the sea.

Taking my place in front of Griff, my smile widened to painful proportions. I couldn't believe how blessed I was, marrying an amazing man that I loved, right next to my best friend, in my favorite place in the world.

"Please bow your heads as we open in prayer," Pastor Dan spoke.

I bowed my head and closed my eyes, inhaling the salty air. Listening to Pastor Dan pray for our marriages, I lifted up my own thanks internally. A droning noise intruded upon the tranquility of the moment.

"Amen."

Straightening after the prayer, I looked for the source of the noise that grew steadily louder. Jet skis.

"We are gathered here today, to witness the joining of these young lives."

My attention strayed from the words being spoken over us. The jet skis raced closer. I gripped my bouquet tightly. They looked like they were coming toward the shore at a dangerous pace. It couldn't even be safe to be in water so shallow, surely.

Evidently, others noticed the joy riders as well. Griff's mouth tightened. Landon squeezed Sam's hand and Pastor Dan raised his voice. The jet skis zoomed nearer still.

"Look out!" BeeBee shouted.

19

Chapter 19

A bang sounded and I ducked, along with everyone else. Smoke began spewing from cannisters tossed onto the sand by the two jet ski riders. My eyes watered. Griff tucked me beside him and bustled me further inland, away from the thick smoke. Our few guests hurried away too, knocking over chairs and slowed down by sand.

Thank goodness for the strong ocean breeze. The wind whisked the smoke away in no time, though the confusion remained. Landon jogged over and captured one of the cannisters seconds before the tide carried it away.

"There's a note," he called.

Our small little wedding party and guests gathered around him.

"What does it say?" Sam asked, leaning over his elbow.

Landon dried the note carefully on his pants. "Here's your smoke bomb. Where's my money?"

He began to crumple the note but something caught my eye. "Wait. There's more on the back."

Sam grabbed the note, reading from the other side. "Next time bang will be bigger."

"We need to call the cops," I said.

Griff squeezed my hand. "Piper, someone else can do that. Let's finish our wedding. Please."

Sam stomped her foot. "I can't believe those jerks tried to ruin our wedding. As if putting Gladys in the hospital wasn't enough."

"Hey y'all," Victoria waved her phone. "Speaking of Gladys. She says you better finish this wedding or she's coming down here to make you herself." Pressing the phone back to her ear, Victoria listened a moment then spoke again. "She also said the wedding video is still recording and that she would call Officer Jack and have him come look at it to see if there is anything that he can use to identify the jet ski jerks."

Everyone righted the overturned chairs and sat.

While the perfect peace of our moment had been shattered, I smiled anyway as I rejoined Griff at the altar. This was a prime example of what marriage was all about. A pair of people who supported one another, lifted each other up after difficulties, and moved forward together.

In no time at all, Pastor Dan closed his Bible, smiled, and said those life-changing words. "You may each kiss your bride."

20

Chapter 20

"What in the world are you doing here?" Gladys slapped the bedcovers. "I swear, young people these days have no common sense. Don't you know you just got married? You are supposed to be at home with your husbands. Do I have to tell you everything?"

Sam arched one thin eyebrow and smirked at the little tantrum.

I put my hands on my hips and tapped a foot. "Are you quite done with the lecture?" I asked.

"That depends on why you're here." Gladys raised her own eyebrows, clearly prepared to engage in a staring contest. Stubborn. Obviously one of my favorite things about her.

"Well, if you're done playing twenty questions, we are here because we have good news."

"You brought cake?"

"Of course." Sam pulled a food container from her enormous shoulder bag. "But that isn't the good news."

"Nope. That's just to celebrate the good news."

"Okay. Tell me?" Gladys leaned forward. "Oh! Did they catch the jet ski dummies?"

"Better. But we'll let Officer Jack explain. He called to tell us and we asked him to wait and meet us here."

Sam put the cake down and pulled out plates and silverware from her bag next. I think maybe she bought it from Mary Poppins, the endless way it held things that shouldn't really all fit.

Three rapid knocks sounded before the door opened. Officer Jack strode in, Griff and Landon behind him carrying several water bottles each.

"Look who we met on the way back from the vending machine." Griff grinned.

Shaking his hand, I thanked Officer Jack for coming all this way. "Please, go ahead and tell us about the case."

"Did you get any leads on the jet skis?" Sam wanted to know

"What about the guy who shot me?" Gladys demanded.

Putting both hands in front of him to wave off any more questions, Officer Jack's chest puffed out in pride and a hint of a smile played across his face for the first time. "As a matter of fact, we got more than leads."

"The arms dealers?" My fists clenched so tightly my nails dug into my palms. I said a silent prayer.

Griff slowly began to massage my shoulders.

"We found the car."

"The car that I damaged the night Gladys was shot?" Landon clarified.

"Yep," Officer Jack nodded again. "Practically the last place we thought we'd find it, too. We searched all of the chop shops and body shops that are known gang hangouts. Nothing. I had some detectives check regular repair shops and one found the car at a really high-end body shop."

Officer Jack accepted a bottle of water from Sam. I bit my tongue; patience was not my strong suit.

"We searched the car and found more weapons. Then, lo and behold, we found a gate key card to one of those swanky neighborhoods not far from old Pirate Pier. Even better, clipped to the visor was a garage door opener. I took the car and a few guys and we drove through the whole neighborhood until we hit on one of those garage doors that worked with the opener. Called in a warrant, kept watch on the place, and by two this morning we had five other men and three teenage boys under arrest. Confiscated enough weapons to finish off a small town." He paused. "I mean it when I say this, thankfully that town won't be ours thanks in part to you ladies. However, I want you all to remember the many ways this could have gone south. Stay out of my investigations in the future. If you don't, I may have to start arresting people."

Officer Jack walked out, leaving us all a bit speechless. Well, almost all of us.

"So, where's the honeymoon going to be? Are you all going together or separately?" Gladys asked gleefully.

Landon turned a shade of pink and Griff laughed out loud.

Sam ignored Gladys in favor of passing out cake.

I looked around at my crazy little family and grinned. It felt good to have things returned to normal again. "I'll take some of that dark chocolate cake!"

Afterword

I'd like to extend a heartfelt thank you to every one of you amazing readers who has journeyed with me through the Ooey Gooey Bakery cozy mystery series.

It has been so much fun getting Piper and Sam in and out of trouble, and exploring their personal lives unfolding right alongside you.

Now, I have some other characters in mind for a few new series clamoring for my attention. That means, I planned this book to be the final in the Ooey Gooey Bakery series.

However, I'm here to serve my readers, so you tell me.

Do you want a few more short stories about mystery and mayhem or honeymoon hijinks?

Click or type the below web address into your browser to answer this quick survey and I'll take your requests into account as I work on my next books this year.

Survey: https://forms.gle/cUezTnC8pLiRnWKH7

About the Author

Katherine Brown is a Texas girl, lover of books, and weaver of words. She has written children's stories as well as cozy mysteries, and dabbles in poetry for personal stress relief. Ice cream and brownie batter are two of her favorite snacks. Katherine and her family live in Texas and enjoy spending time together, watching movies, and hiking / exploring beautiful scenery on vacations.

You can connect with me on:

🌐 http://katherinebrownbooks.com

🔗 https://instagram.com/katherinebrownkatie

Subscribe to my newsletter:

✉ https://mailchi.mp/5cd1e0a6e2e0/kbbnewsletter

Also by Katherine H. Brown

Visit https://www.amazon.com/Katherine-Brown/e/B078J72H8M for all of the books by Katherine H. Brown.

Bonbon Voyage

Gladys is going on a cruise! Her new husband insists on all the finest. But it isn't all fun and games on board the boat. Not when Gladys witnesses a man fall overboard. Was it an accident? Or was it murder? Armed with wigs and wits, Gladys plans to find out.

Becky Beats the Mean Girls
Middle grade fiction.

I'm Becky.

The new girl.

Again.

Dad's work keeps us moving a lot, so I'm sort of used to it. Still, being the new girl in middle school for the umpteenth time isn't exactly easy. And to make things worse, the mean girls AKA Thing One and Thing Two, already have it out for me on day one.

Good thing I have a plan to beat them.

I've been tweaking it for years in every school I've been to.

Time to test it, and myself, out for real.